D1434815

for Lauren Stone

British Library Cataloguing in Publication Data
A catalogue record for this book is available from the British Library

ISBN 0 340 65602 6 Hardback
ISBN 0 340 68149 7 Paperback

Copyright © Hilda Offen 1997

The right of Hilda Offen to be identified as the Author of the Work
has been asserted by her in accordance with the
Copyright, Design and Patents Act 1988

10 8 6 4 2 3 5 7 9

First published 1997
by Hodder Children's Books,
a division of Hodder Headline plc,
338 Euston Road, London NW1 3BH

Printed in Hong Kong

THERE MIGHT BE GIANTS

Hilda Offen

Hodder
Children's
Books

a division of Hodder Headline plc

"Sally! Joe!" said Mum. "You'd better get ready.
We must go into town right away."
"I'll get the dressing-up box," said Joe.

"Just your coats will do," said Mum.
"We need to dress up properly," said Sally.
"You never know who we'll meet on the way."

"There might be giants," said Joe, "or dragons."
"Get a move on," called Mum. "The market closes at four."

"But we need the right outfits," said Sally.
"What if we meet a monster?"
"Or a wizard!" said Joe. "There might be wizards about."

"Stuff and nonsense!" said Mum. "Come on,
we're going. Now!"
"We're ready," said Sally.
"Ready for anything!" shouted Joe.

"I've never known such slow children," said Mum.
"Giants indeed!" she grumbled.
"There are no such things."

"Are you sure, Mum?" asked Sally.

"Quite sure," said Mum.

Mum grumbled on and on.

"As for dragons – what rubbish!" she said.
"Dragons aren't real."

"But if they were," said Joe, "I bet they'd be scary."

"You'd have to think fast with a dragon about," said Sally.

"And fancy being frightened of monsters!"
snorted Mum.

"Huh! Monsters are just make-believe,"
she said.

"They don't frighten us," said Sally.

"No way," said Joe.

"Good, that's the shopping done," said Mum.
"Now we can go home for tea."

She started to laugh.
"And you can stop worrying about wizards," she said.
"I've never seen a wizard in my life."

"You'd have to be quick to spot one," said Sally.

"They move very fast," said Joe.

"Well – that was a really ordinary walk," said Mum.
"Not a giant or a dragon in sight. No monsters
or wizards either."

"It's a good thing we wore our outfits," said Joe.
"Come on," said Sally. "Let's look at
our collection."

Labels in image: Wizard's hat, Monster's ribbon, Giant's button, Dragon's scale

When it was time for bed they snuggled down
and Mum kissed them goodnight.
"Sleep tight," she said. "And remember – there are no
giants outside! No dragons! No monsters! No wizards!"

"We know!" said Joe.
"Do you know how we know?" whispered Sally.
"Tell me," said Mum.
"WE FRIGHTENED THEM ALL AWAY!"
shouted Sally and Joe.